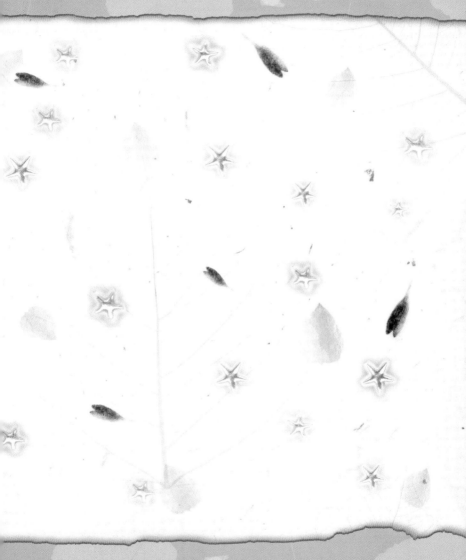

W9-CSU-139

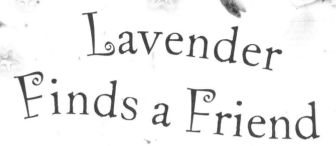

Lavender
Finds a Friend

Based on the Original Flower Fairies™ Books
by Cicely Mary Barker

Frederick Warne

Hidden amongst the leaves
and blossoms in the garden,
the Flower Fairies live quietly.
At night, they come out to play!

In the morning, a sleepy Lavender
is the first to wake up. She has
lots to do! She sings to the
other garden fairies,
to wake them up, too!

Lavender's blue diddle, diddle—
Lavender's green;
I'll scent the clothes diddle diddle
Put away clean—
Clean from the wash, diddle diddle,
Hanky and sheet;
Lavender's spikes,
diddle diddle,
Make them all sweet.

When Lavender
has a minute to spare,
she writes in
her diary.

Dear Diary
Today I have been busy
washing the fairies' clothes.
I have made some
soft lavender soap

and I scrub away at the stains. I wonder what some of the fairies get up to – their clothes are so dirty!

Once Lavender finishes washing
the fairies' clothes, she hangs them
up on the line to dry.
"Your bonnet is beautifully scented!"
says Sweet Pea Fairy to her sister.

One day, in the garden,
Lavender hears two fairy
friends laughing together.

14

"I wish I had a best friend of my own," Lavender thinks.

That evening
Lavender writes
in her diary...

Dear Diary

I'm sad tonight.
Every day I wash an
scent the fairies' cloth
but I never have

time to make
any friends. My only
friends are the white
butterflies who visit each day
to drink Lavender nectar.

Whatever shall I do?

"I know what I'll do, I'll make
a friendly fairy spell,"
says Lavender.
This is what
she puts in it:

a dash of
fairy dust

a whisper
of moon sparkle

a drop
of dew

a tiny fairy
giggle

a sprinkle of
Lavender petals

Lavender casts the
spell and waits to see
who will come…

Out steps Cornflower from the
flower bed. "I'll be your friend!" he says.
"Me too!" calls Foxglove from behind her.
"And me," says Snapdragon.
Lavender laughs. "What a wonderful
spell!" she says.

FREDERICK WARNE

Published by the Penguin Group
Penguin Books Ltd, 80 Strand, London WC2R 0RL, England
New York, Australia, Canada, India, New Zealand, South Africa

This edition first published by Frederick Warne 2006
1 3 5 7 9 10 8 6 4 2

This edition copyright © Frederick Warne & Co., 2006
New reproductions of Cicely Mary Barker's illustrations
copyright © The Estate of Cicely Mary Barker, 1990
Copyright in original text and illustrations
© The Estate of Cicely Mary Barker 1923, 1925, 1926,
1928, 1934, 1940, 1944, 1946, 1948
All rights reserved.

ISBN 0 7232 5186 X

Printed in China